Bamboo Hats and a Rice Cake

a tale adapted from Japanese folklore

BY ANN TOMPERT   ILLUSTRATED BY DEMI

CROWN PUBLISHERS, INC.   *New York*

For Stacie, my Japanese connection,
with many thanks for her help
— A. T.

Di Zang Wang Pu Sa
—Demi

A note to parents and teachers:

In Japanese, the same character is used to indicate both

singular and plural. Thus, 餅 can mean both "rice cake"

and "rice cakes," 扇 both "fan" and fans," and so forth.

Text copyright © 1993 by Ann Tompert
Illustrations copyright © 1993 by Demi

Published by Crown Publishers, Inc., a Random House
company, 225 Park Avenue South, New York, New
York 10003

CROWN is a trademark of Crown Publishers, Inc.

Manufactured in Singapore

Library of Congress Cataloging-in-Publication Data
Tompert, Ann.
    Bamboo hats and a rice cake: a tale adapted from
Japanese folklore / by Ann Tompert ; illustrated by
Demi.
    p.   cm.
    Summary: Wishing to have good fortune in the new
year, an old man tries to trade his wife's kimono for
rice cakes.
    [1. Folklore—Japan.] I. Demi, ill. II. Title.
PZ8.1.T57Bam 1993
398.21—dc20
[E] 92-26849

ISBN   0-517-59272-X (trade)
       0-517-59273-8 (lib. bdg.)

10 9 8 7 6 5 4 3 2 1   FIRST EDITION

rice cake

餅

ong ago there lived in the mountains of the Land of the Rising Sun an old couple who had no children. They were poor, and one year the snows came so early that things were harder than usual for them. By the time the Great Last Day of the year arrived, they had scarcely a grain of rice to eat.

"Never before have we celebrated the New Year without 餅," said the old man.

rice cake

餅

kimono

着物

"If we sold my wedding 着物 at the village market, we could have 餅 for New Year's Day and many days after," said the old woman.

"Sell your wedding 着物!" protested the old man. "We can't do that. It was your mother's wedding 着物 and her mother's before that."

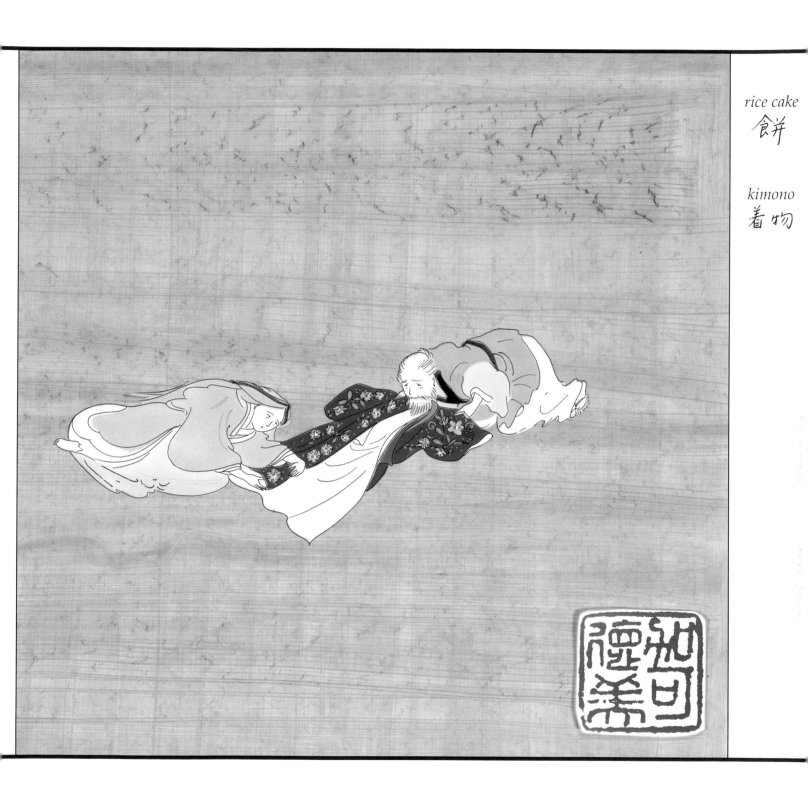

rice cake
食餅

kimono
着物

"But we should eat 食餅 for at least the first three days of the New Year if we want good fortune to smile on us," said the old woman.

"It is a hard choice," said the old man, sighing. But he could think of nothing else to do, so he reluctantly agreed.

rice cake

餅

kimono

着物

With the 着物 carefully packed in a basket strapped to his back, he set off down the snow-covered mountain trail to the village.

After walking for some time, the old man reached a shrine where there stood six statues of Jizo, the protector of children, covered with snow.

The old man clapped his hands three times and bowed.

rice cake

食并

kimono

着物

"Oh, dear," he said. "You must be cold standing in the snow."

And he brushed the statues clean.

"Forgive me," he said after he finished. "I do not have anything to offer you. But I'm on my way to the village market to sell my wife's wedding 着物 to buy 食并. I'll leave some for you on the way back."

He bowed again before going on his way.

rice cake
餅

kimono
着物

fan
扇

The old man had not traveled far when he met a neighbor coming up the trail with a basket of 扇.

"Any luck at the market today?" asked the old man.

The woman shook her head. "No," she said. "I had hoped to sell enough 扇 to buy a 着物."

"Oh," said the old man. "It happens I have a 着物 to sell."

And he showed the woman his wife's 着物.

"It's beautiful!" exclaimed the woman. "Worth many 扇. I wish I could buy it, but..."

She shrugged her shoulders, sighed, and started up the trail.

rice cake
餅

kimono
着物

fan
扇

"Wait," said the old man. "I can see you really want this 着物 . Why don't we trade? I will give you the 着物 for your 扇."

"Do you really want to?" asked the woman.

The old man bowed. "If it will make you happy," he said.

Thanking the old man, the woman took the 着物 and went on her way.

rice cake
餅

kimono
着物

fan
扇

The old man traveled down the trail until he reached the village. There he found the market filled with people swarming about like bees.

Holding up several 扇, the old man walked up and down the market.

rice cake
餅

kimono
着物

fan
扇

" 扇 for sale," he called as loudly as he could. "Beautiful 扇 for sale."

But the hurrying, scurrying crowd ignored him. No one even glanced at the 扇 .

rice cake
餅

kimono
着物

fan
扇

noodles
そば

By and by the old man grew hungry.

"Perhaps I can trade a 扇 for something to eat," he thought.

He approached a man selling そば from a two-wheeled cart.

"M-m-m-m," said the old man, closing his eyes and sniffing, "your そば smell so good."

"Do you want some?" asked the そば peddler.

rice cake
餅

kimono
着物

fan
扇

noodles
そば

"Will you trade a bowl of そば for a 扇?" asked the old man.

"A bowl of そば for a 扇!" cried the そば peddler. "Tell me. What would I do with a 扇 in winter?"

He laughed, and everyone nearby began to laugh, too. Hanging his head, the old man crept away.

rice cake
餅

kimono
着物

fan
扇

noodles
そば

He was so flustered that he did not notice the roly-poly gentleman who was following him.

"Wait a minute," called the roly-poly gentleman, tugging the old man by the sleeve. "I'll take all your 扇."

"All of them?" exclaimed the old man.

The roly-poly gentleman nodded. "If you will take this little gold 鈴 for them."

"Surely I will have no trouble selling a gold 鈴," the old man thought. "Everyone needs a 鈴 to ring in the New Year. And a gold 鈴 should ring in much good luck."

And he agreed to trade.

rice cake
餅

kimono
着物

fan
扇

noodles
そば

bell
鈴

bamboo
hat
笠

The roly-poly gentleman left with the basket of 扇, and the old man once again trudged up and down the market.

"鈴 for sale," he called again and again while ringing the little gold 鈴. "Ring in good luck with this golden 鈴."

But it was late in the afternoon. The crowd in the market had thinned out. Those who were left ignored the old man with his little gold 鈴. It began to snow. Tired and discouraged, he decided to go home. It was then that he happened upon a young man selling 笠.

rice cake
餅

kimono
着物

fan
扇

noodles
そば

bell
鈴

bamboo hat
笠

"Have you sold many 笠 today?" asked the old man.

"No," said the 笠 seller, sighing. "My luck has not been good. I have sold only three 笠." He sighed again.

"I'm sorry to hear that," said the old man.

The 笠 seller straightened his sagging shoulders. "But I hope to sell them all," he declared. "There is still time."

rice cake
食餅

kimono
着物

fan
扇

noodles
そば

bell
鈴

bamboo
hat
笠

As they talked, a feeling of fatherly concern for the 笠 seller filled the old man's heart. "Maybe my gold 鈴 will change his luck," he thought.

"I want to buy some of your 笠 with my gold 鈴," he said.

"But why?" asked the 笠 seller.

The old man shrugged.

rice cake
餅

kimono
着物

fan
扇

noodles
そば

bell
鈴

bamboo hat
笠

"What will you do with them?" asked the 笠 seller.

The old man shrugged again. He could not bring himself to express his feelings.

"All right," said the 笠 seller, handing the 笠 to the old man. "I hope you don't regret this."

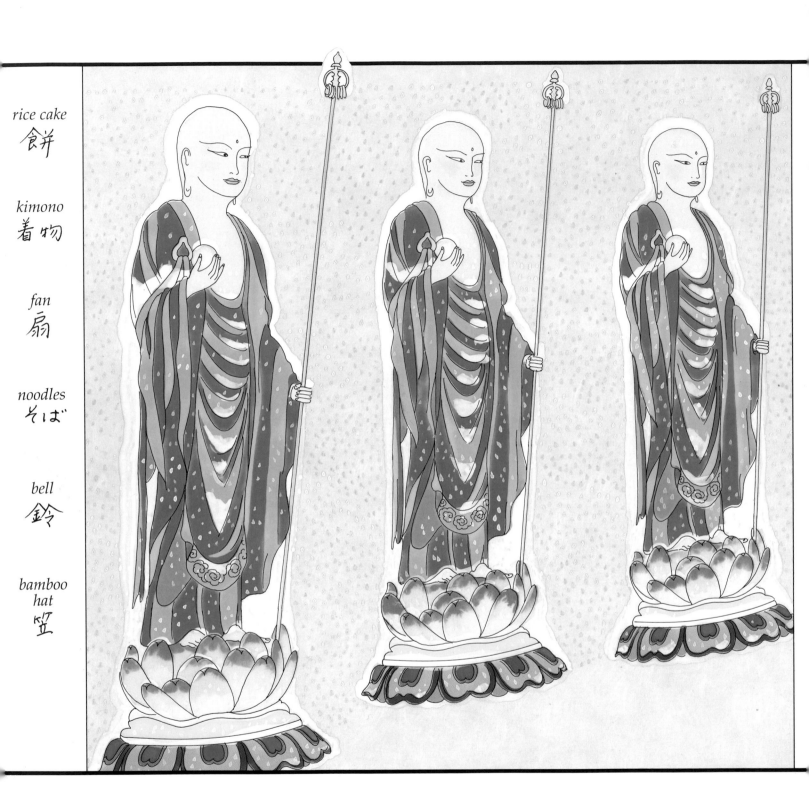

rice cake
餅

kimono
着物

fan
扇

noodles
そば

bell
鈴

bamboo hat
笠

Carrying the 笠 on his back, the old man headed home. The snow fell faster and faster. By the time he reached the six statues of Jizo, they were all covered with snow again. The old man clapped his hands three times and bowed.

rice cake
餅

kimono
着物

fan
扇

noodles
そば

bell
鈴

bamboo hat
笠

"I'm sorry," he said. "I couldn't buy 餅, so I can't leave you an offering."

He started to brush the snow from the statues.

"This won't help you much," he said. "You'll soon be covered with snow again. I wish I had some umbrellas to give you."

rice cake
餅

kimono
着物

fan
扇

noodles
そば

bell
鈴

bamboo
hat
笠

Then he remembered the 笠. One by one he tied them to the heads of the statues.

"Now, at least your heads won't get so cold," he said.

rice cake
餅

kimono
着物

fan
扇

noodles
そば

bell
鈴

bamboo hat
笠

When he reached the sixth statue, he discovered that he had only five 笠. He took off his own 笠 and put it on the statue's head. And bareheaded, he set off up the mountain trail again.

rice cake
餅

kimono
着物

fan
扇

noodles
そば

bell
鈴

bamboo
hat
笠

When he reached home, the old man looked like a walking snowman.

"You must be frozen to death!" cried the old woman. "What happened to your 笠?"

And while he sat by the fire thawing out, the old man told her how he had traded her 着物 for some 扇 and the 扇 for a little gold 鈴 after he had tried without success to get some そば for a 扇, and how he had exchanged the 鈴 for the five 笠.

"Then, on my way home," he said, "I put the 笠 on the Jizo statues to keep the snow off their heads."

rice cake
食餅

kimono
着物

fan
扇

noodles
そば

bell
鈴

bamboo hat
笠

"And because you had only five 笠," concluded the old woman, "you gave *your* 笠 to the sixth Jizo statue."

The old man nodded. "I'm sorry that I didn't bring back any 食餅," he said.

"You did something much better when you showed kindness to the Jizo statues," said the old woman.

"Do you really think so?" asked the old man.

"Of course," said the old woman. "I'm proud of you."

rice cake
餅

kimono
着物

fan
扇

noodles
そば

bell
鈴

bamboo
hat
笠

By this time it was very late, so the old man and the old woman went to bed. A while later they were awakened from a deep sleep by a loud thud.

"What was that?" cried the old woman.

"I don't know," cried the old man.

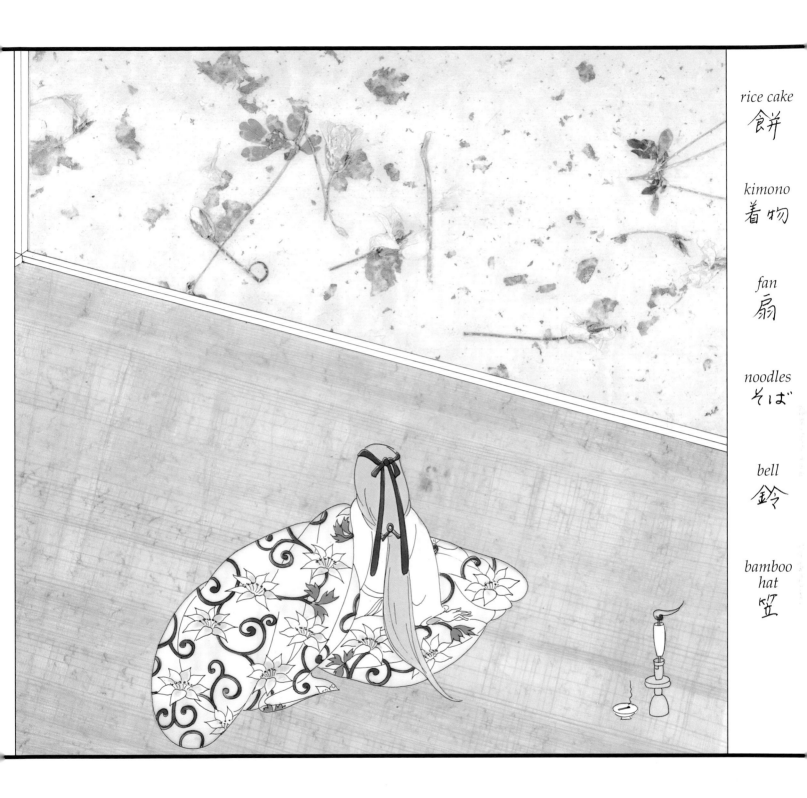

rice cake
餅

kimono
着物

fan
扇

noodles
そば

bell
鈴

bamboo
hat
笠

They jumped out of bed, crept to the front door, opened it, and peeked out.

rice cake
餅

kimono
着物

fan
扇

noodles
そば

bell
鈴

bamboo
hat
笠

"Look at this!" gasped the old man.

There on the doorstep, resting on a straw mat, was an enormous 餅.

"Where did it come from?" the old woman wondered aloud.

rice cake
餅

kimono
着物

fan
扇

noodles
そば

bell
鈴

bamboo
hat
笠

Looking about, they spied the six Jizo statues a short distance away, tottering off in single file.

The statue bringing up the rear stopped, turned, and bowed to the astonished couple.

rice cake
餅

kimono
着物

fan
扇

noodles
そば

bell
鈴

*bamboo
hat*
笠

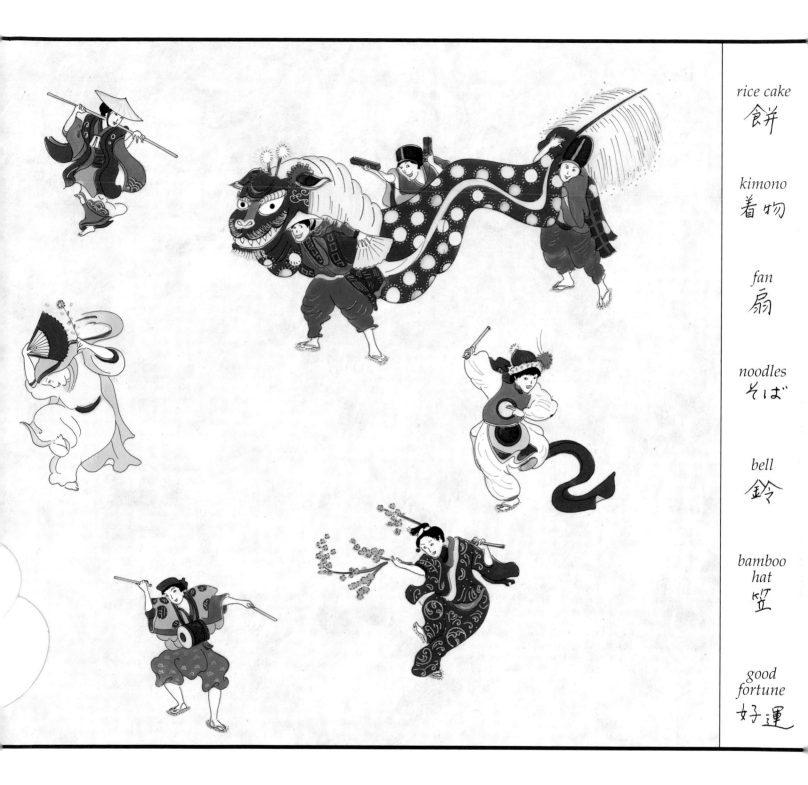

What a wonderful New Year's celebration the old man and the old woman had the next day!
The 餅 that the Jizo statues left on their doorstep kept them well fed for a long time. And
好運 smiled on them that year and all the years of their lives.

Author's Note

The Japanese welcome the New Year with great seriousness. Traditional foods, including a two-tiered round rice cake, play a prominent part. People generally eat rice cakes for at least the first three days of the New Year to bring good fortune.

In one form or another, rice has worked its way into most corners of Japanese life. It is used to make rice gruel, rice wine, rice starch, and rice paste. Rice straw is made into mats for homes, ropes, sacks, and wrappings of various kinds. Many communities hang rice ropes in Buddhist shrines to acknowledge their dependence on rice.

Jizo is the most gentle divinity of the Japanese Buddhist faith. According to ancient Japanese Buddhist beliefs, when children die, they must cross the River of Three Roads to reach paradise. A gruesome witch stands guard at the river. She shows the children piles of stones and tells them that if they build towers that are high enough, they will reach paradise. However, the witch and her followers knock down the towers as fast as the children can build them. Jizo, the protector of children, chases the witch and her followers away and hides the children in the sleeves of his kimono. Statues of Jizo are often surrounded by little piles of stones, left by visitors to help the children build their towers.

Over the years, many tales have been told about Jizo and statues of him. *Bamboo Hats and a Rice Cake* was adapted from one of them.

—A. T.

Illustrator's Note

In Oriental art and bookmaking, placing the Heaven and the Earth is the first essential for creating harmony: Open space above is the Heaven shining through; open space below is the Earth's solid foundation. Between is the placement of Man, where all life moves.

In *Bamboo Hats and a Rice Cake*, this law of placement and design is used throughout: the Heaven above, the Earth below, and the pictures of Man in between. In Japanese art, this Buddhist law is known as *ten chi jin*, or Heaven, Earth, and Man. This law pervades the universe. It means that nothing is without its Heavenly origin. The painted subject is not executed without its Heavenly reference, nor is the object, nor are the details. Understanding this totality, the work is rounded to completion.

—Demi

rice cake
(mochi)
餅

kimono
(kimono)
着物

fan
(ōgi)
扇

noodles
(soba)
そば

bell
(suzu)
鈴

bamboo hat
(kasa)
笠

good fortune
(kōun)
好運